THE RUNAWAY ROLLER SKATE

also by John Vernon Lord (with Janet Burroway)

THE GIANT JAM SANDWICH

The Runaway Roller Skate

Verses and pictures by John Vernon Lord

Piper Books
in association with Jonathan Cape

for Tara, Kirstine, Anna and Hilary

Into the country far away
Mr Ellwood went on a holiday.
To roller skate was his delight;
If possible, from morn till night.

The thing that he most loved to do
Was to skate in the country, admiring the view.

Then one sunny morning, at ten to eight,
A mouse crept into his roller skate.
"Giddy-up," it squeaked. Off went the mouse,
Through a hole in the door, and out of the house.

The cat, who had no sense of smell,
Slept soundly, thinking all was well.
But the cockerel woke: "Cock-a-doodle-doo!"

Mr Ellwood cried, "Oh, it can't be true!
It's terrible! It's infuriating:
It will mean the end of my roller skating.'

The jockey-mouse rode with his bootlace reins;
Mr Ellwood banged on the window-panes,
Shouting, "Catch that mouse before it's too late,
He's got my irreplaceable roller skate."

Mr Ellwood, frantic, all of a rumpus,
Picked up his telescope and his compass,
A lasso, mousetrap, clothes-peg and chain,
A map and umbrella (in case of rain),
A butterfly net, among other things,
And paraphernalia dangling on strings.

He asked a fisherman fishing for trout
If he'd seen a roller skate dashing about.
"Shssh! Can't you see that I'm trying to fish
For something tasty to put in my dish?
Have a look in the river; maybe it's there.
Take yourself off, please. Don't stand and stare."

Mr Ellwood decided to do something rash:
He jumped in the river with a mighty splash.
"I say, Mr Fish, has a mouse passed by,
Riding a roller skate (heaven knows why)?"
The fish flipped his fins, and gaped, "Bubble, bubble."
Mr Ellwood thanked him for all his trouble
And advised him to keep well away from the bait
Lest he finish his days on a dinner plate.

And down the river they travelled so fast
That the ducks flapped away to let them past.
"Come on now," the cockerel squawked, "heave-ho.
I'll steer the boat, you'll have to row."

They rowed out to sea and tossed on the ocean.
The waves swirled high — there was such a commotion:
The wind blew and whistled, and down the rain poured
FLASH! struck the lightning; the thunder roared

They arrived at a desert, in scorching heat,
And mounted a camel — each hump made a seat.
Mr Ellwood croaked, all thirsty and hot,
"Look, *there* goes the mouse . . . or maybe not . . ."

Though his teeth were chattering in the ice and snow,
"I don't care", Mr Ellwood said, "*how* far we go.
I'll climb frozen hills on that mouse's track,
I'll search till I get my roller skate back."

After many a month of constant chase
It seemed to them that they'd lost the race,
When just as they rested their aching feet
The skating mouse rushed down the street.
"Taxi, taxi, follow that skate!
Quick, oh quickly, before it's too late!"

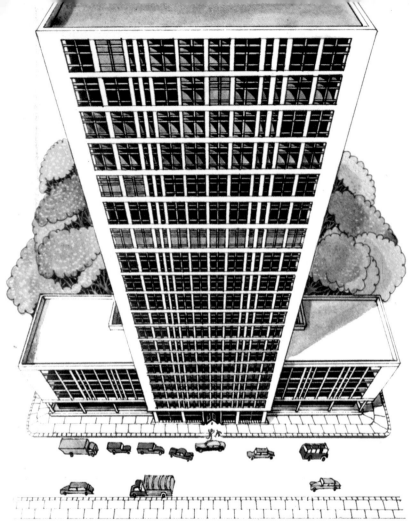

With a terrible sound of screeching wheels
The cab pulled up at the mouse's heels.
They chased him through rotating doors
Into a building of twenty floors.

Mr Ellwood asked the girl in the hall
If he might make a telephone call.
Without looking up she said, "Yes, but sign
Here first above the dotted line."

He started each call, "Sir, strange to relate,
I'm looking for a runaway roller skate."
Each man he rang passed him on to another,
Until someone said, "You want Big Brother."

"Big Brother is the boss in the office upstairs:
No one ever sees him, and no one cares."
Mr Ellwood glimpsed the mouse across the floor
Run down a passage and through a door.

He rushed to the room, where sat a stern man.
In a trembling voice Mr Ellwood began,
"Dear sir, please help me, I'm in such a state.
A mouse has gone off with my roller skate."
"I'll assist if I can, but I'm terribly busy.
I do nothing all day but it makes me feel dizzy.
Now, let me see – 'A mouse on a skate'.
Sharpen my pencils and I'll put you straight."

The pencils were heaped all over the floor,
Big ones, little ones – oh, what a chore!
He must have sharpened nearly a million,
Black ones, green ones, purple, vermilion,
When outside the window a dart glided past
With the mouse and the roller skate tied on fast.

The cock and Mr Ellwood didn't turn a hair:
They jumped from the window out into the air.
Down and down and down they sailed
Till even Mr Ellwood's stout heart quailed.
The cockerel's feathers flapped and fluttered.
Gripping his gamp, Mr Ellwood spluttered,
"It's the landing, dear cock, that I really dread.
Oh, how I wish I had stayed in bed!"

Their luck that day was extremely good.
They touched down safely in the middle of a wood.
They asked an owl who was perched in a tree
If he knew where the mouse might possibly be.
He blinked and hooted, "To-wit-to-woo,
I would go that-a-way, if I were you.
"You'll come to a castle where, I'm told,
Lives a kindly man who is wise and old."

With their scissors and sword they snipped and hacked
Through the forest growth and tangled track.

They struggled and cut their way through the wood
And came to a clearing where a castle stood.
Around its walls was a deep, wide moat,
Filled with many a yawning crocodile throat.

Having read the notice, Mr Ellwood decided
To clean their teeth with the paste provided.
So he diligently scrubbed the crocodile teeth,
Brushing up and down, above and beneath.

In the castle they met a strange old man.
Feeling rather shy, Mr Ellwood began:
"Excuse me, sir, I hope I'm not too late.
Have you seen a mouse on a roller skate?"
The ancient replied with prompt decision,
"We can track his course on that television.
Please accompany me. It's not very far.
We can travel on foot. We don't need a car.

"See, the mouse has gone to that house on the hill.
If you make haste he should be there still."
Mr Ellwood thanked him for being so kind,
For mice on roller skates are hard to find.

"Look," crowed the cockerel, "that's *our* house.
Let's hurry up and catch that troublesome mouse."
"Well," said Mr Ellwood, "I think you're right.
We'll be able to sleep at home tonight."

Look! There's the skate on the bedside mat;
The mouse isn't there, only the cat.
"Never mind the mouse I had hoped to capture,
I've found my skate, what joy and rapture!"

At last Mr Ellwood went to bed,
Glad to rest his weary head;
But suddenly the poor man woke,
Crying aloud, "Is this a joke?
Good heavens, what on *earth* is that
Tiptoeing across the mat?
Oh no! Alas, what grief and pain —
IT'S THAT MEAN AND MEASLY MOUSE AGAIN!"